200143943

Lmd
kendailvue

D1712776

Alvin the Knight

Alvin the Knight

by Ulf Löfgren

Carolrhoda Books, Inc./Minneapolis

Alvin loved museums. They were full of such exciting things!
Jeweled crowns, Egyptian mummies, Model T cars, and Plains
Indian arrowheads were just a few of the things that sparked
Alvin's imagination.

One day Alvin went to the museum and found himself in the
knights' hall. A huge statue of a knight stood in the center of the
room. He was dressed in full armor with a sword, a shield, and a
big banner. Another knight sat on a stuffed horse.

What splendid knights they are! thought Alvin.

I'd like to become a knight, wished Alvin. If I had a big horse and my own sword and shield, I could compete in tournaments and topple my opponents with my lance, and win fabulous . . .

CREEEEK. An old wooden door opened and interrupted Alvin's dreaming. A boy in strange clothes peered out and beckoned to Alvin. "You there, hurry up! We've no time to lose. We're already late," he whispered nervously.

Alvin followed the boy through the door and down into a dark cellar. Some mice watched them from the bottom of the stairs.

"The others have been waiting ages for us," scolded the boy. "But you simply cannot wear that ridiculous cap!"

"Hang that silly thing on the hook over there," suggested the boy. "I have a proper hat and cloak for you instead. Now we'd better get moving, or we'll catch it for dawdling."

The boys passed through another small doorway, while a cat chased away the mice from beneath their feet.

All of a sudden, Alvin was in a field, staring at a strange and colorful parade.

"Get a move on. We've waited long enough! Sir Justus wants to leave," scowled a large man holding a sharp-looking halberd.

Then a finely dressed man on a horse, with a sword hanging from his belt, commanded, "We shall have to hurry if we're to make it in time for the feast!" Alvin was sure the man was a *real* knight.

"You can ride behind me on my horse," said the boy to Alvin.

"My name is Felix," the boy explained after Alvin climbed up behind him. "The big knight in blue is Sir Justus, and I'm his squire. I take care of Sir Justus's horses and armor. Sir Justus's family is riding behind us. Of course, they're all talking about tomorrow's tournament."

What tournament? wondered Alvin.

In the distance, Alvin saw a great castle. "Sound the trumpets!" ordered Sir Justus. The herald blew a loud, ringing note on his horn, and the drawbridge opened like a huge mouth.

"I expect you'll begin by lending a hand in the kitchen," said Felix to Alvin. "This afternoon there's to be a big feast in the castle, so there'll be plenty to do."

Kitchen work just isn't what I had in mind, thought Alvin.

Alvin was taken directly to
the kitchen. "Aha . . . so you're
the new kitchen boy, are you?"
said the cook when he caught
sight of Alvin. "You look a bit on the
scrawny side, but we can always
find something for you to do."

"As a matter of fact," ventured Alvin, "I had hoped to become
a knight."

"A knight!" roared all the kitchen folk. "Ho ho ho, ha ha ha!"

"So the young scamp wants to become a knight," laughed the
cook. "What next . . . what next?"

"Well, Sir Alvin," snorted the cook with a laugh, "you can start by bringing in some wood. We need lots of wood for our big stoves. And when you finish with that noble deed, you can fetch some water . . . at least ten pails."

"Gee," sighed Alvin, as water splashed onto the stone floor. "I must be the lowliest servant in the land."

"Hey Alvin! Hurry over
with that big cauldron," cried
one of the kitchen boys.
Alvin heaved the iron pot
over to the stove without
spilling any of the soup that
was inside.

"Sweep up around the big
stove," added one of the girls.
"It's a terrible mess!" With a
few quick swats of his broom,
Alvin cleared away the dust
and grime.

"Sir Justus wants his apple cider . . . NOW!" shouted the cook. "Deliver his mug to him immediately."

"I'm on my way," answered Alvin as he dashed off, his cloak billowing out behind him.

"Put silken cushions on all the benches," shouted the cook, "for the feast will soon begin." Alvin ran hither and thither with armfuls of cushions.

After the feast started, Alvin worked even harder.

Knights and ladies came from miles away for the feast. Alvin carried out enormous plates overflowing with food. Great jugs of juice were poured for all the thirsty guests. Everyone ate and drank to their hearts' content. Even the castle dogs ate their share.

After dinner the musicians started to play, but the music could barely be heard over the clanking of glasses and other festive noises. "We need another drummer," one musician cried, "and another piper too."

"I can manage that," Alvin announced. Alvin dropped his platter and grabbed a drum and pipe. He began to play them both at the same time, while the crowd hooted and hollered with delight.

"More! More! Let's have more entertainment!" called out Sir Justus. Alvin picked up five balls and juggled them over his head. The balls whirled up into the air and back down without once falling to the floor.

"Just look at that!" exclaimed Sir Justus. "That lad seems to be able to do most anything. Felix! Lend Alvin a suit of armor and a lance. Then show him how to use them."

"Certainly, Sir Justus," replied Felix.

"Alvin is indeed a talented boy," Sir Justus whispered to his daughter Daphne. "I want to see how he fares in some knightly tasks." Daphne nodded in agreement.

"You can borrow a lance from me," said Felix. "Then we'll see
if you can mount Fitznagel. But I might as well warn you . . .
I'm pretty good at jousting."

Alvin wasn't afraid. He climbed onto Fitznagel and poked
Felix in the stomach with his lance. Felix lost his balance and fell
off his horse! Sir Justus and Daphne looked on, pleased with
Alvin's success. Only poor Felix was disappointed.

ALVIN MAY MEET HIS MATCH YET!

"You shall become one of my knights," proclaimed Sir Justus. He paraded down to the field and tapped Alvin on the shoulder with his broadsword. "I dub you Sir Alvin. And what shall be the symbol of your knighthood?" he asked, as a crowd watched from the castle.

"My blue-spotted cap!" Alvin declared proudly.

"Then your banner, shield, and horse's smock shall all bear that symbol," said Sir Justus. "Tomorrow the great tournament will begin, and we shall see how you get on. But don't get the notion that jousting is a nursery game. Oh no, indeed!"

The next day, large crowds gathered
to watch the tournament. Everyone
wondered how the jousting would go
for the new knight, Sir Alvin.

The trumpet sounded at last, and the tournament began. Alvin flipped down the visor on his helmet and raised his lance. He gave Fitznagel an encouraging nudge, and they bolted into the mass of other knights.

Alvin thrust his lance to the left and then to the right, and treated the crowd to a great surprise—down went all the other knights, bump, bump, bump. Soon a great pile of floundering, armored men sat jumbled in the dirt.

"Hooray!" shouted Daphne.

"Hooray!" cheered the crowd.

Unfortunately, this made the other knights very angry. They scrambled to their feet and tried to grab Alvin.

Alvin dropped his lance and fled. Even without Fitznagel, he was too fast for the other knights.

YOU CAN'T ESCAPE, ALVIN!

Alvin ran until he reached a door. He could hear the knights right behind him. He pushed the door open...

... and dashed down some stairs, throwing off his helmet and armor.

At the bottom of the stairs was a small passageway.

Alvin crouched down and crawled through the opening.

He grabbed it and peeked around
an old wooden door at the top
of the stairs.

"Hooray," gasped Alvin when
he spied his blue-spotted cap.

. . . he rushed up three
flights of stairs, tossing off
the rest of his armor as
he went.

When Alvin reached the
other end . . .

He hoped he wouldn't run into anything in the dark.

Alvin caught his breath and looked around. He was back in the museum again! "What a relief," Alvin muttered.

A man in a green uniform was staring curiously at him. "That door is supposed to be locked," the museum guard said gruffly, and he locked it with one of the big keys hanging from his belt.

"That's fine with me," said Alvin as he walked away. "I don't think I'd ever *dare* become a knight again."

This edition first published 1992 by Carolrhoda Books, Inc.

Originally published by Norstedts Förlag, Stockholm.
Original edition copyright © 1989 by Ulf Löfgren under the title
ALBIN RIDDARE.
All rights to this edition reserved by Carolrhoda Books, Inc.
No part of this book may be reproduced, stored in a retrieval
system, or transmitted in any form or by any means, electronic,
mechanical, photocopying, recording, or otherwise, without the
prior written permission of the Publisher except for the inclusion
of brief quotations in an acknowledged review.

Library of Congress Cataloging-in-Publication Data

Löfgren, Ulf.
    [Albin riddare. English]
    Alvin the Knight / by Ulf Löfgren.
        p.   cm.
    Translation of: Albin riddare.
    Summary: When Alvin visits a museum and sees an exhibit of
medieval costumes, he is suddenly drawn into an imaginary adventure
where he gets the opportunity to prove his skill as a knight in a
medieval land of kings and castles.
    ISBN 0-87614-698-1
    [1. Knights and knighthood—Fiction. 2. Civilization, Medieval—
Fiction.] I. Title.
PZ7.L826Aj   1992
[E]—dc20   91-16398
                                                            CIP
                                                            AC

Manufactured in the United States of America

1 2 3 4 5 6 7 8 9 10 01 00 99 98 97 96 95 94 93 92